A Nasty Plan

Jessica was getting an idea.

"Maybe we could fix it so the new teacher doesn't want Mrs. Otis's job," she said thoughtfully.

"What do you mean?" Lila asked.

"We can act like rascals," Jessica said.

Todd began to smile. "Yeah. If we're really rotten and horrible, she won't want to be our teacher."

Elizabeth stared at Jessica. "Is that what you mean? You think we should be bad on purpose? When Mrs. Otis asked us to be good?"

Jessica crossed her arms and looked seriously at her sister. "Do you want Mrs. Otis to get kicked out?"

Bantam Books in the
SWEET VALLEY KIDS series

SWEET VALLEY KIDS

GET
THE
TEACHER!

Written by
Molly Mia Stewart

Created by
FRANCINE PASCAL

Illustrated by
Ying-Hwa Hu

BANTAM BOOKS
NEW YORK • TORONTO • LONDON • SYDNEY • AUCKLAND

To Joshua Spencer Stein

RL 2, 005-008

GET THE TEACHER!
A Bantam Book / February 1994

*Sweet Valley High® and Sweet Valley Kids are
trademarks of Francine Pascal*

Conceived by Francine Pascal

*Produced by Daniel Weiss Associates, Inc.
33 West 17th Street
New York, NY 10011*

Cover art by Susan Tang

ISBN: 0-553-48106-1

Published simultaneously in the United States and Canada

*Bantam Books are published by Bantam Books, a division of Bantam
Doubleday Dell Publishing Group, Inc. Its trademark, consisting of the
words "Bantam Books" and the portrayal of a rooster, is Registered in
U.S. Patent and Trademark Office and in other countries. Marca
Registrada. Bantam Books, 1540 Broadway, New York, New York 10036.*

PRINTED IN THE UNITED STATES OF AMERICA

CWO   9 8 7 6 5 4 3 2 1

CHAPTER 1

A Special Guest

"I wonder who our surprise visitor is going to be," Jessica Wakefield said, jumping off the last step of the bus at Sweet Valley Elementary. "I hope it's a famous movie star."

"Or an astronaut," said her twin sister, Elizabeth. Their teacher, Mrs. Otis, had told them to expect a surprise guest next Monday, and Elizabeth was already tingling with curiosity.

"It doesn't matter who it is," Jessica said confidently. "I bet they won't be able to tell us apart!"

Elizabeth knew that was true. Most people couldn't tell her apart from Jessica since they weren't just twins—they were *identical* twins. Both girls had blue-green eyes and long blond hair with bangs, and they both wore name bracelets on their wrists. When they dressed exactly alike, even their best friends were glad the name bracelets gave them an easy way to tell who was who.

Those similarities were only on the outside, however, because inside, each girl had her own special personality. Jessica liked modern-dance class and playing with her dolls. Elizabeth preferred playing soccer with her friends or reading. She especially liked animal and mystery books.

But even though they were different in many ways, they were still best friends. They shared a bedroom, and they shared toys, and they could often finish each other's sentences. Elizabeth thought that an identical twin sister was the best kind of sister in the world.

Hand in hand, they walked to their second-grade classroom and stopped at the closed door. Inside, they could see students rushing back and forth and could hear them screaming and shouting directions.

"That way! They went that way!" Winston Egbert yelled, pointing toward the back of the room.

"They're going to get my lunch!" Caroline Pearce whined, standing on her chair.

Elizabeth giggled as she and Jessica quickly entered the room. "Did the hamsters get loose?" she asked Sandy Ferris.

"Yes, Thumbelina went that way, and Tinkerbell went the other way," Sandy said, getting down on her hands and knees to look under the teacher's desk.

Todd Wilkins threw himself across the floor as if he were sliding into home plate. He had his baseball glove open for a catch. "I got one!" he said.

"Be careful!" Amy Sutton cried out. "You'll squish her!"

"All right, everybody, settle down," Mrs. Otis said, coming into the room. "I know it's Friday, but it's not the weekend yet."

She clapped her hands, and one by one, the kids stopped running around. They climbed off their chairs and desks and got up from the floor. They stopped laughing and shouting and squealing and began to take their seats. Eva Simpson reached down carefully and picked up the second hamster. Very quietly, Todd and Eva put the hamsters back into their cage.

"Now, that's more like it," Mrs. Otis said with a smile as the class came to order. "I thought I had come to the Sweet Valley Zoo by mistake."

Mrs. Otis opened her attendance book and began to call out names.

"I have a few announcements," she said when she finished. "First, remember we're having our Valentine's Day party at the end of next week."

"Super," Jessica whispered to Elizabeth. "I hope I get a lot of cards."

"And most important," Mrs. Otis continued, "the special guest I told you about will be joining us first thing on Monday morning."

Elizabeth sat on the edge of her seat.

"A young woman who just graduated from teachers college will be our student teacher all next week," Mrs. Otis said. "I'll expect each and every one of

6

you to be polite, cooperative, and help-ful. This will be her first time as a student teacher, and she'll be very nervous. I know you'll treat her with the same respect you show me."

"We'll be on our best behavior," Caroline said in her most goody-goody prim and proper voice. She was always trying to butter up to the teacher.

Elizabeth smiled. Having a young student teacher sounded fun. She couldn't wait for Monday.

CHAPTER 2

Taking Over

At recess that day, Jessica saved a seesaw for herself and Elizabeth. Lila Fowler, Jessica's best friend after Elizabeth, got on the next seesaw with Ellen Riteman.

"I think it'll be fun to have a student teacher, don't you?" Jessica said to her friends as Elizabeth climbed on the other end of her seesaw.

"Don't you understand what that means?" Lila asked. "I think it's terrible."

Jessica pushed herself up into the air. "What does it mean?"

Lila shook her head slowly back and forth in a mysterious way. She always wanted people to think she knew more than they did.

"Yeah, Lila, what's so terrible about it?" Elizabeth asked impatiently.

"You figure it out," Lila said. "We're having a brand-new *young* teacher come in. And Mrs. Otis is *old*."

"So?" Ellen asked.

"Don't you see?" Lila said, her voice rising. "The new teacher is going to take over for Mrs. Otis."

Jessica got a funny feeling in her stomach. And it wasn't from coming down on the seesaw. "No way," she said nervously. "Mrs. Otis would never leave Sweet Valley Elementary. She's been here forever."

"Well, now she's getting kicked out," Lila said matter-of-factly.

By this time, several other students from their class had gathered around to listen.

"What makes you so sure, Lila?" Ken Matthews asked.

Lila looked around proudly. She loved having an audience. "Remember Mr. Hinkley, the fifth-grade teacher? He was old, and they kicked him out. Now Mrs. Lombardo teaches that class."

Ken nodded, as did everyone else.

"Even if that is true," Elizabeth said, "it doesn't mean they're kicking out Mrs. Otis. She isn't *that* old."

Lila shook her head. "I saw this movie on TV last night where the exact same thing happened. There was a big movie star who got all the best parts. But she got older, and a pretty young actress pushed her out so she could be the star."

Amy Sutton sat on the ground with a

worried frown on her face. "What if Lila's right?" she asked.

"What if the Valentine's Day party is really a good-bye party for Mrs. Otis?" Jessica asked in a frightened whisper.

Ellen began to sniffle. "But Mrs. Otis is the b-b-best teacher in the w-w-world!" she cried. "I love her."

"Me too," Jessica agreed, feeling her own eyes fill up.

"We all do," Elizabeth said. "She's the nicest and smartest and best teacher ever."

Todd punched his fist into his base-ball glove. "We can't let this happen," he said angrily.

"We could do something," Winston said. "We could change the sign that says Sweet Valley Elementary to some-thing else, like Sweet Valley Dog Pound. That way, when the new teacher comes, she'll think she's in the wrong place and she'll leave."

"Or we could all go to the principal's office and beg Mrs. Armstrong to let Mrs. Otis stay," Eva suggested.

Jessica looked toward the windows of their classroom. The panes were covered with construction-paper hearts. Her heart had *raccoon* written on it.

But now she was getting an idea. *Raccoon* made her think of the word *rascal*.

"Maybe we could fix it so the new teacher doesn't want Mrs. Otis's job," Jessica said thoughtfully.

"What do you mean?" Lila asked.

"We can act like rascals," Jessica said.

"What?" Lila demanded.

"Hey, I get it," Todd said, beginning to smile. "If we're really rotten and horrible, she won't want to be our teacher."

13

Elizabeth stared at Jessica. "Is that what you mean? You think we should be bad on purpose? When Mrs. Otis asked us to be good?"

Jessica crossed her arms and looked seriously at her sister. "Do you want Mrs. Otis to get kicked out?"

"No," Elizabeth answered.

"Then we have to do it," Jessica said firmly. "It's as simple as that."

The kids standing around the see-saws all nodded. Starting Monday morning, they would act like monsters.

CHAPTER 3

Out of Control

Elizabeth and Jessica looked at each other nervously as they entered their classroom on Monday morning. They both wore blue jeans, white T-shirts, and white sneakers, and they both had their hair in a ponytail with a pink ribbon. Neither one was wearing her name bracelet.

"Sit in my seat," Jessica whispered.

Elizabeth nodded. Standing at the blackboard was a young, pretty woman with long blond hair. Elizabeth looked away quickly.

"Class," Mrs. Otis began once everyone was seated. "I'd like to introduce you to Ms. Kovac."

"Hi," Ms. Kovac said cheerfully. "I'm very pleased to meet you all. I'm sure we're going to have a great week together."

Just then, a bright red rubber ball bounced toward the front of the room from the back. Nobody spoke as the ball hit the blackboard with a *ka-bump*.

"Hey, this is great," Ms. Kovac said, catching the ball and tossing it up in the air. "I can add this to my collection."

Elizabeth and Jessica shared a worried look. It seemed as though Ms. Kovac was not easy to upset.

Mrs. Otis looked at the class and frowned slightly. She walked over to Ms. Kovac and handed her the class book. "Why don't you take attendance?

That's a good way to get to know the students. I have to go to the principal's office, but I'll be right back."

"Fine," Ms. Kovac said, opening the book as Mrs. Otis left. "Now, when I take attendance, I like to start in the middle. Lila Fowler?"

"Here," said Ellen.

"She's not Lila," Caroline interrupted. "She's Ellen Riteman."

Ellen stuck out her tongue at Caroline. "I thought she said my name."

"That's okay, Ellen," Ms. Kovac replied with a smile. "I'll mark you present. Now, how about Lila?"

Lila waved her hand in the air. "Sorry," she said in an unapologetic voice. "I didn't hear you the first time."

"That's all right," Ms. Kovac replied. "Andy Franklin?"

"Here," Andy said, knocking a stack

of notebooks and papers off his messy desk. The papers flew across the floor in a big *whoosh*. Andy got down on his hands and knees to pick them up. As Ms. Kovac bent over to help him, three paper airplanes sailed through the air.

"Ms. Kovac?" Charlie Cashman asked in a loud voice. "Can I go to the bathroom?"

"Oh, of course," Ms. Kovac said, standing up with a handful of Andy's papers.

"Ms. Kovac?" Sandy said, whining a little bit. "I feel sick. I think I might throw up."

Instantly, Jessica let out a bloodcurdling shriek. "I'll throw up too if I see her throw up!" she cried.

"Oh, please don't!" Ms. Kovac begged. "What's your name?"

"Liz Wakefield," Jessica said.

"No, I'm Liz," Elizabeth spoke up.

"No, I'm Liz," Jessica said. "She's Jessica."

Elizabeth nodded.

"They're not in their correct seats," Caroline said.

Elizabeth and Jessica both stood up to switch seats, but then they stood up again and switched, and then again. Behind them, some kids were giggling.

"I have a question!" Winston said.

"Yes?" Ms. Kovac asked quickly. "What is it?"

"Uh . . . I forgot," Winston said.

"Let's switch again," Jessica whispered.

Elizabeth nodded, and they quickly stood up and ran around their desks three times and sat back down in the same seats just as Mrs. Otis returned.

"How is everything?" Mrs. Otis asked.

"Just fine," Ms. Kovac said, trying to sound convincing. She looked somewhat relieved that Mrs. Otis was back.

"Elizabeth and Jessica, please sit in your proper seats," Mrs. Otis said. She could always tell the twins apart.

Elizabeth couldn't look Mrs. Otis in the eye as she traded places with Jessica. She had never been so rude before, and she felt bad. But she reminded herself that it was all for Mrs. Otis.

For the next few minutes, everyone behaved perfectly as Ms. Kovac finished taking attendance. Then the student teacher sat on the edge of the front desk.

"Let's talk about Valentine's Day," Ms. Kovac began eagerly. "It's my favorite holiday of the year, because it's also my mother's birthday. That always makes it seem extra special to me. Who else likes Valentine's Day?"

21

Nobody spoke. Jessica scribbled a note, folded it up, and threw it to Lila. "Pass it on," she whispered loudly.

Mrs. Otis frowned at Jessica, but didn't say anything. She watched as the note was thrown around the room. Obviously, she was letting Ms. Kovac run things.

"Oh, it's only a piece of paper," Ms. Kovac said brightly as she picked up the note, which had fallen to the floor near her. "I was afraid someone had let a bug in. Now, who can tell me their favorite thing about Valentine's Day?" Ms. Kovac said as she sat down again on the edge of the desk.

Elizabeth was beginning to wonder if their plan would work. No matter how badly behaved they were, Ms. Kovac remained cheerful and friendly all morning. She never lost her temper or even stopped smiling.

"Please turn in your extra-credit projects if you have them," Mrs. Otis said before recess.

All the kids were hurrying out to the playground as fast as they could. Elizabeth took a report out of her notebook and carried it to the teacher's desk.

"What's this?" Ms. Kovac asked. "You're Elizabeth, right?"

Elizabeth looked at the ground. "Yes. It's a story."

"A story? Great!" Ms. Kovac said. "I enjoy writing stories myself. I'll read this one right away." She smiled. "Do you want to give me a hint of what it's about?"

Elizabeth gulped. "No," she muttered, and hurried outside.

CHAPTER 4

Making New Friends

Jessica stood at the center of a group of her classmates on the playground. She felt like the commander-in-chief of an army.

"What can we do to Ms. Kovac after lunch?" she asked. "Any ideas?"

"How about letting the hamsters loose?" Ken suggested. "Maybe Ms. Kovac will be afraid of them."

"OK," Jessica said. "But make sure she doesn't step on one of them by accident."

Elizabeth was frowning. "I don't

think she'll be afraid of Tinkerbell and Thumbelina," she said.

The others nodded in agreement.

"Maybe someone could catch a bee!" Winston said hopefully. "Then we could let it loose."

Jessica grinned. It was fun to be naughty on purpose. "That's not bad enough," she said. "Let's think of something really awful."

"You're all going to get in trouble!" Caroline said.

Everyone turned around in surprise. "Who said you could spy on us?" Lila demanded.

"I just heard you, that's all," Caroline said. "And I'm telling Mrs. Otis that you're being mean to Ms. Kovac on purpose."

"Don't you dare!" Jessica said, grabbing Caroline's arm.

25

"Just remember, Caroline," Lila broke in. "Ms. Kovac isn't the only one we can be mean to."

Caroline's eyes widened. "Umm . . ." She fiddled with a button on her shirt and scuffed her feet on the ground. "OK. I won't tell."

"Good," Jessica said, smiling slyly at Lila.

"Come on," Todd said, waving the others into a huddle. "Let's think of something really bad for this afternoon."

After lunch, Jessica dawdled back to the classroom. She was having a lot of fun misbehaving. She took her seat as Mrs. Otis asked for attention.

"I'm going to leave Ms. Kovac in charge for a little while," she said, giving the class a stern look. "And please have better manners than you did this morning."

Everyone smiled and nodded, as if to show that they were the best and most helpful second graders in the world. Then Mrs. Otis left the room.

"All right, kids," Ms. Kovac said. "Please turn to page twenty-seven in your reading books. This is a story called 'Making New Friends.' Who would like to start reading out loud?"

Jessica put up her hand. "May I, Ms. Kovac?" she said politely.

"Of course!" Ms. Kovac looked very pleased.

Jessica turned to page seven in the book and read a poem called "The Bubble Bath." Several students laughed behind their hands.

"That's the wrong page, Jessica," Ms. Kovac said gently.

"Oh, I'm sorry," Jessica said, trying to look sad.

"Let me read," Todd volunteered.

Ms. Kovac nodded. "OK. Go ahead."

Todd cleared his throat. "Ahem," he coughed. Then he began reading in a slow, uncertain voice. "*Mmmmm-mmm*— is that word *making*?"

"Yes," Ms. Kovac said encouragingly.

Todd nodded and squinted at the page. "Making *nnnn-nnnn*—is that word *new* or *no*?"

"*New,*" Ms. Kovac said. Her smile was fading.

"Making new *ff-ffff*—" Todd scratched his head, and Jessica couldn't help giggling.

"*Friends,*" Ms. Kovac said curtly. "Making New Friends."

"Oh, right," Todd said. "Making No Friends."

Ms. Kovac sighed and asked Andy to

continue reading. Todd glanced over at Jessica and Lila and gave them a thumbs-up sign. It looked as though their plan was beginning to work.

CHAPTER 5

A Crummy Teacher

The Wakefields had barbecued chicken and french fries for dinner that night, Elizabeth's favorite. She sat down at her place, licking her lips. Just as she was about to dig in, Mrs. Wakefield brought up the one subject Elizabeth didn't want to think about.

"So, how is the new student teacher working out?" their mother asked as she poured a glass of milk for Jessica.

"Just fine," Jessica said. "She's working out great."

Elizabeth's appetite fizzled away. She

put down her fork and stared at her french fries. All she could think about was how many tricks they had played on Ms. Kovac that day. She felt bad, even though no matter what they did, Ms. Kovac never seemed to get upset. Elizabeth could picture the student teacher, with her long blond hair and her cheerful expression as she took Elizabeth's story to read. It would have been so much easier to be mean if Ms. Kovac hadn't been so nice.

"How do you like her, Liz?" Mr. Wakefield asked.

"Oh, well . . ." Elizabeth shrugged. She loved Mrs. Otis, but the truth was, she liked Ms. Kovac, too. She avoided Jessica's eyes. "She's OK, I guess."

"No, she's not," Jessica said, frowning hard at Elizabeth. "She's not OK at all."

Steven, the twins' fourth-grade

brother, shook his head at Jessica. "A second ago you said she was great."

"Uh, what I meant to say is that our plan is working great," Jessica said.

"What plan?" Mrs. Wakefield asked.

Elizabeth picked up a french fry and nibbled the end. She looked nervously at her sister. Their parents would certainly not approve of scaring Ms. Kovac away, even if they knew it was to keep Mrs. Otis from being replaced.

Jessica was looking at their parents with a very innocent expression on her face. "Our plan for getting to know Ms. Kovac," she explained.

"I see," their mother said. "Do you think she's a good teacher?" she asked Elizabeth.

"She's a lousy crummy teacher!" Jessica shouted before Elizabeth could even answer.

"Really?" Mr. Wakefield looked surprised. "She's a crummy teacher? I'm surprised the school would have a student teacher who wasn't any good."

Mrs. Wakefield put her elbows on the table. "Is there any particular thing that she's doing wrong?"

"Well . . ." Elizabeth said hesitantly. "It's hard to say. She's only been here one day so far."

"So what?" Jessica said. "She could be here for a million-and-one years, but she'd still never be as good a teacher as Mrs. Otis."

Elizabeth nibbled at her french fry again. She was feeling very sorry for Ms. Kovac.

"Right?" Jessica said, nudging Elizabeth with her elbow. "She'll never be as good a teacher as Mrs. Otis."

"I guess not," Elizabeth agreed.

She tried hard to push Ms. Kovac's picture out of her mind. Instead, she imagined Mrs. Otis and was glad they'd be able to keep her.

CHAPTER 6

Splash!

On Tuesday, Jessica and Lila and Todd met next to the hamster cage before attendance.

"I brought some rubber spiders," Todd said, digging into his pocket. One had a black body and purple legs. The other was green with orange specks. "Where should I put them?"

"In Ms. Kovac's hair," Lila whispered.

"Eeew!" Jessica shivered. "That's horrible."

"I know," Lila said with a smile.

Jessica glanced back over her shoulder. Ms. Kovac was talking to Mrs. Otis by the front windows. She tried to imagine Ms. Kovac jumping from fright and screaming "SPIDER!" Jessica wrinkled her nose.

"I think that's too mean," she said.

"Maybe I'll just put them on her chair or something," Todd said. "I'll think about it."

Jessica felt a shiver go up and down her spine—spiders anywhere sounded horrible. Then she reminded herself not to feel sorry for Ms. Kovac.

"Class," Ms. Kovac said, coming to the center of the room with her usual cheerful smile. "Let's spend art class this morning making Valentine's Day cards for each other. I'll collect them all in a box and then hand them out at the party on Friday."

There was a noisy rush as everyone

ran to the large art tables at the back. Ms. Kovac selected three people to help pass out markers, paints, brushes, and construction paper, and soon each student was busy working.

"What are we going to do to her today?" Ellen asked in a whisper, swishing her paintbrush around in a cup of water.

"Whatever you do, don't volunteer for anything," Lila ordered. "If she wants someone to help clean up, don't say anything."

Jessica nodded. "And make a really big mess if you can."

"I can," Ellen said confidently.

Jessica swirled her own paintbrush around in the pink paint and sloshed the brush across the table, leaving a wet pink streak. Around her, kids were talking and laughing or telling secrets about who their valentines were for. Ms. Kovac stood at the back of the room by the sink, carefully washing her hands.

Jessica looked around. There was a feeling of suspense in the classroom. Everyone was waiting for something big to happen. Just then, Lois Waller picked up a cup of dirty paint water and began walking slowly toward the sink. Lois was often teased for being chubby. She was also a bit of a klutz.

"Psst. Look over there," Jessica said, nudging Lila and pointing at Lois.

Lois's cup was filled to the brim with dirty black paint water, and Lois was being so careful, and concentrating so hard, that her tongue stuck out of the corner of her mouth.

"Psst," Lila whispered, nudging Ellen.

Ellen looked at Lois and nudged Todd. Todd nudged Ken, and Ken nudged Sandy.

Jessica held her breath as Lois drew closer and closer to Ms. Kovac and the sink. Just before Lois reached the counter, Charlie stuck his foot out into the aisle and tripped her.

"Whooaaaa!" Lois yelled, lunging forward.

Ms. Kovac turned around just in time to see the cup of paint water fly toward her.

"No!" she gasped. The water splashed all over her hair, her pink sweater, and her yellow pants.

The room fell totally silent.

"Oh, I'm so sorry!" Lois wailed. "I'm so sorry, Ms. Kovac. I didn't mean to do it!" She began crying.

"Don't cry, Lois," Ms. Kovac said. She smiled faintly as she tried to wipe off her clothes with some paper towels. "I know you didn't mean to do it. It was an accident."

Mrs. Otis hurried to the back of the room. "Here, let me help you," she said, clucking her tongue in sympathy. She looked at the class. "Go on back to work, everyone. You too, Lois."

As the two teachers tried mopping off Ms. Kovac's clothes, Jessica strolled over to the counter to set her painting out to dry.

"I'm sure this will come off at the dry cleaners," she heard Mrs. Otis say.

"Oh, I guess, but I was hoping to wear these clothes a few more times before I had to get them cleaned," Ms. Kovac said sadly. "This is the only new outfit I bought especially for student teaching."

Jessica hurried back to her table and repeated what she had heard.

"I don't think Ms. Kovac even cares that much about the job," Lila said.

"If teaching was really important to her, she would have bought a whole bunch of outfits for school instead of just that one."

They looked at Ms. Kovac's stained clothes and smeared makeup, and both of them started to giggle. "Our party on Friday really *is* going to be a good-bye party," Jessica whispered. "A good-bye party to Ms. Kovac!"

CHAPTER 7

The New Kid in School

Over the next two days, the students in Mrs. Otis's class acted like perfect monsters. No one raised a hand to answer questions. Whenever Ms. Kovac called on someone, that person asked her to repeat the question, and then deliberately answered it wrong. They all talked out of turn and refused to stay in their seats. Elizabeth was beginning to wonder how much longer they could keep it up.

"It's time for music," Ms. Kovac said on Thursday morning. "Will someone please get the songbooks from the back closet?"

Elizabeth looked around. Nobody volunteered, not even Caroline. Ms. Kovac drew in a deep breath, and let it out slowly. Her smile quivered.

"Anyone?" Ms. Kovac asked in a sad voice.

Elizabeth's cheeks turned pink. She felt terrible for poor Ms. Kovac. Ms. Kovac always tried so hard.

"Todd, how about you?" Ms. Kovac asked.

Todd slumped in his chair. "Aw, do I have to?"

"Yes, please," Ms. Kovac said, trying to sound cheerful.

Elizabeth doodled on her notebook, feeling embarrassed. They had been so awful all week that their plan was sure to work. There was no way Ms. Kovac would want to stay at Sweet Valley Elementary. But, Elizabeth told herself, Ms. Kovac was probably a good teacher and would have no trouble finding a job at a different school.

I hope, Elizabeth thought, crossing her fingers.

The music lesson was a disaster. Everyone began singing at different times. They sang in different keys, and some people even sang the wrong song. Elizabeth heard Jessica giggle and wondered if everyone except her was having a good time being so bad.

After music, Ms. Kovac asked the class to write stories. They separated into their writing groups, then spent a long time sharpening pencils and ripping sheets of paper out of their notebooks. When everyone was finally working, Ms. Kovac walked over to

Elizabeth's desk and smiled at her.

"I'm looking forward to reading your story, Liz," Ms. Kovac said. "I really enjoyed the one you gave me on Monday."

"Oh, thanks," Elizabeth muttered. She looked around to see if anyone was listening. Jessica was frowning at her and shaking her head as if to say, *Don't cooperate*.

"Let me know if you need any help," Ms. Kovac said to Elizabeth before walking to another group.

"What did she say to you?" Jessica whispered.

"She said she thinks I'll write a good story," Elizabeth whispered back.

Jessica shook her head. "Well, don't. Write the stupidest story in the world, OK?"

"But, Jess . . ."

"Do you want Mrs. Otis to stay or don't you?" Jessica hissed.

Elizabeth gulped. "I guess you're right."

She gripped her pencil tightly in her hand, and then began writing. For ten minutes, the room was silent as the students wrote their stories. Mrs. Otis and Ms. Kovac walked around, helping different kids with their writing and answering questions. But each time one of them passed near Elizabeth, she covered her work with her hand so they couldn't see it. At last, Ms. Kovac asked for a volunteer to read out loud.

"I will," Elizabeth said, raising her hand.

She stood up. Jessica gave her a warning look as she walked to the front of the room. "My story is called 'The New Kid in School,'" Elizabeth began. "A new girl came to school and tried to make friends with everyone. But nobody

liked her. 'Why don't you like me?' she asked. 'Because we don't want you here,' the other children told her. She was sad, but she decided to go to a different school. The other kids all cheered when she left. The end."

There was a startled silence in the classroom. Elizabeth raised her eyes from her paper. Ms. Kovac was staring at the floor, and Mrs. Otis was looking at Elizabeth with an expression of disappointment and sadness on her kind face.

"That's not what I expected from you, Elizabeth," Mrs. Otis said quietly. "Not what I expected at all."

Elizabeth could feel her eyes filling with tears. She had never been so ashamed in her life. She hurried back to her seat and didn't look up again until Ms. Kovac dismissed the class for recess.

CHAPTER 8

A Secret

"I'm not being mean to Ms. Kovac anymore," Elizabeth said as soon as they reached the playground. "It's not right. I really disappointed Mrs. Otis."

Eva nodded. "Ms. Kovac looked pretty sad, too."

Jessica looked at the group. "Listen. You guys can't give up now. We've been doing so well. There's no way Ms. Kovac will want to stay. It's too bad that Mrs. Otis is upset about it, but it's for her own good. Besides, tomorrow's Friday and our jobs will be done."

With a firm nod, Jessica headed for the swing set.

"Jessica, your shoelace is un—" Elizabeth began.

It was too late. Jessica tripped over her shoelace and fell on her hands and knees. "Ooowww!" she howled. "My hand!"

There was a bad scrape on her left hand, and small bits of dirt and sand were stuck in the cut.

"Does it sting?" Elizabeth asked.

Jessica blew on it and blinked away the tears in her eyes. "I'm going to the nurse," she sniffed.

She tied her shoelace and ran into the building. The halls were empty and quiet, since everyone was out on the playground. As Jessica passed the teachers' lounge, she heard a familiar voice.

"Hi, Mom." It was Ms. Kovac's.

Jessica peeked through the open

door. Ms. Kovac stood with her back to Jessica, talking on the telephone. There was no one else in the room. Jessica flattened herself against the wall outside the door, hoping to hear something that would help the plan to get rid of Ms. Kovac.

"This just isn't working out the way I thought it would," Ms. Kovac said. Her voice sounded tired and unhappy. "I can't seem to get through to these kids at all, no matter how hard I try."

Jessica nodded in satisfaction.

"All I ever wanted was be a teacher," Ms. Kovac went on. "But now it looks like I'll never be able to. The way my student-teaching assignment is going, no one will ever offer me a job."

A hot flush ran across Jessica's face.

"I don't know what I'm going to do," Ms. Kovac said. Her voice shook with every word. "How will I pay back my college loans if I can't get a job?" She sniffed.

Jessica's stomach sank all the way to her sneakers. She wished she had not stopped to spy. She decided to try to forget everything she had just heard and tiptoed away from the open door. Then she ran the rest of the way to the nurse's office.

"I need a bandage," Jessica said breathlessly, holding out her hand.

The nurse patted the examination bench. "Hop up here," she said. "I'll get something to clean that scrape." As Jessica sat on the bench, the nurse pulled a privacy screen in front of her. Jessica sat swinging her legs and blowing on her hand.

There was a soft knock on the nurse's door. "Excuse me, Ms. Simon, do you have any aspirin? I have a terrible headache."

Jessica froze. It was Ms. Kovac's voice. She could believe Ms. Kovac had a headache, with the way things had been going all week.

"Of course," the nurse said. "I'll be right with you. I just have to take care of someone else first."

"Can I help?"

"Sure. It's one of your own students," the nurse told her.

Ms. Kovac followed the nurse to the bench and saw Jessica. Jessica stared at her.

"Oh, Jessica," Ms. Kovac said with a warm smile. "Did you hurt yourself?"

"Yes," Jessica whispered.

"Poor thing," Ms. Kovac said. She sat on the bench next to Jessica and looked at Jessica's hand. "If it stings when the

nurse cleans that scrape, you can scream as loud as you want. I promise I won't tell anyone."

Jessica felt a lump in her throat. Even though she had been mean to Ms. Kovac from the beginning, the student-teacher was being really nice. Just then, the nurse dabbed a cotton ball wet with peroxide on the cut, and Jessica burst into tears.

"Does it sting?" Ms. Kovac asked.

"Yes!" Jessica lied. It didn't sting at all, but she felt terrible. And when Ms. Kovac gave her a hug, she felt even worse.

CHAPTER 9

Change of Plans

Elizabeth finished the last problem of her math homework and put down her pencil. She looked across the bedroom at Jessica. Her sister was lying on her bed, staring into space.

"What's wrong, Jessica?" she asked. "You've been moping since we got home. You can't stare at the ceiling forever."

Instead of answering, Jessica rolled over and buried her face in the pillow.

"Jess? What is it?"

"Uhf-uh-ammmfffuff," came Jessica's muffled voice. Elizabeth grabbed her stuffed koala bear and sat on the edge of Jessica's bed. Her sister rolled over again and stared at her miserably.

"Please tell me," Elizabeth said.

Jessica sniffed. "I—I heard Ms. Kovac talking to her mother on the phone in the teachers' lounge today," Jessica said. "She's afraid she'll never be able to be a teacher and that she'll never get a job. And she owes money from going to college."

Stunned, Elizabeth dropped her koala bear on the floor. "What?" she whispered.

"We've been so mean to her, and all she ever wanted was to be a teacher," Jessica said with a sob in her throat. "We've ruined everything."

"Oh, no!" Elizabeth said. "I knew this whole thing was a terrible idea. What if she *doesn't* get a job, all because of us?"

Jessica wiped her eyes. "What can we do now? There's only one day left until she leaves."

"We'll just have to be the best students ever," Elizabeth decided. "Just like Mrs. Otis asked us to at the beginning. That way, Mrs. Otis will be proud of us, and Ms. Kovac will know she really is a good teacher and she'll get to be one."

"You don't think it's too late?" Jessica asked doubtfully.

"I sure hope not," Elizabeth answered, jumping off the bed. "Come on. We can start by calling people on the phone."

Together they ran down the stairs and burst into the den.

Elizabeth's heart was pounding as Jessica grabbed the telephone ahead of her and dialed Lila's number.

"Lila, we have to stop being mean to Ms. Kovac," Jessica blurted as soon as

Lila answered. "It was all a huge mistake, and if we aren't super-nice to her, we'll ruin her life. Promise to be nice tomorrow, OK? Call Ellen and pass it on." Jessica hung up before Lila could say anything.

Elizabeth took the phone and called Amy and Todd, and then Jessica called Winston and Sandy. Elizabeth sat biting her thumbnail, thinking hard.

"I have an idea," she announced.

Jessica hung up the telephone. "What is it?"

Elizabeth smiled. She thought she knew a good way to make up for all the mean things they had done to Ms. Kovac. She hurried out of the den. "You'll see!"

On Friday morning, Elizabeth and Jessica stopped at Mrs. Otis's desk when they got to school. A large, pink-wrapped box with a slot in the top sat on the desk. An arrow pointed to the slot, and thick, sparkly letters spelled out VALENTINE MAILBOX.

Jessica slipped several cards into the box, and Elizabeth took the ones she had made out of her notebook. Then she took one extra-large card out of her book bag and shoved it through the slot.

"Who's that one for?" Jessica asked, her eyes wide. "I bet it's for Todd."

"Nope," Elizabeth said with a giggle. "It's for someone really special."

Through the open door, Elizabeth saw Ms. Kovac headed for their classroom. The student teacher walked slowly, without her usual cheerful smile. Elizabeth put her hand behind her back and crossed her fingers.

She just hoped they weren't too late.

CHAPTER 10

A Surprise Valentine

Ms. Kovac opened the attendance book and cleared her throat. "Winston Egbert?" she said, starting in the middle.

"Here."

"Lila Fowler?"

"Here."

Ms. Kovac looked surprised to hear them answer so promptly. She read through the class list, and each student raised his or her hand and sang out "Here!"

"Would anyone like to write this

week's spelling words on the black-board?" Ms. Kovac asked doubtfully when attendance was finished.

Jessica waved her hand in the air. "Can I?"

Ms. Kovac smiled. "Okay—Elizabeth?"

"I'm Jessica," Jessica told her politely.

Mrs. Otis nodded, and Ms. Kovac looked relieved. "Go ahead, Jessica."

When it was time for reading, six kids volunteered to read aloud.

"That's terrific," Ms. Kovac said. She watched the class with a worried look, as though she expected something terrible to happen.

But nothing happened all morning. The only unusual thing was that Jessica volunteered to do a long addition problem on the blackboard.

"Do you think she's any happier?"

Jessica whispered to Elizabeth as she sat down again.

"I hope so," Elizabeth whispered back. "Everyone is acting even better than they do for Mrs. Otis!"

Yet even though the students were behaving perfectly, Jessica never saw Ms. Kovac's sunny smile all morning. It seemed as though the student teacher had given up hope of getting along with the class.

Before the recess bell rang, Mrs. Otis stood at the front of the room. "Now, we could all go outside and play," she said. "Or we could stay inside and do homework."

"Boo!" the class yelled. They all knew she was joking.

"Or we could stay here and have a Valentine's Day party!" Mrs. Otis said.

"Party!" Jessica shouted, jumping out of her seat.

"Perhaps we can get some volunteers to help Ms. Kovac pass out napkins and paper cups," Mrs. Otis continued. "Who would like—"

"Me!" Lila called.

"I will!" Todd said, his hand shooting into the air.

"I'll help!" Winston offered.

The three of them rushed from their seats to gather around the student teacher.

Startled, Ms. Kovac looked from one volunteer to the next. "Th-thank you," she stammered with a hint of a smile.

Jessica sat on the edge of her seat, eagerly waiting for a cupcake. Soon everyone had candy hearts and cherry punch, and Mrs. Otis picked up the card mailbox.

"What's in here?" Mrs. Otis asked, shaking the box next to her ear.

Everyone grinned, but nobody answered.

"Oh, well, I guess I can throw this away," Mrs. Otis said.

"No!" the class shouted.

Laughing, Mrs. Otis opened the box and began calling out names. One by one, students went to the front of the room to receive their valentines. Although Jessica received a whole bunch of valentines, she was still curious to know who would get the enormous card that Elizabeth had made.

At last, Mrs. Otis drew Elizabeth's large card from the box and opened it. "My goodness," she said. "This gigantic one is for Ms. Kovac."

Everyone quieted down and turned

to look at Ms. Kovac. "For me?" she asked in surprise. She slowly walked forward and took the card from Mrs. Otis. "'We really like you, Ms. Kovac,'" she read. "'From the whole class.'"

Jessica looked at Elizabeth and felt her heart swell with pride. Elizabeth always had the best ideas.

The room was silent. Ms. Kovac shook her head again and again. "I can't believe it," she said. "This is so wonderful. Thank you."

"But we still love Mrs. Otis best," Elizabeth said.

"That's right," Jessica added. "And we don't want Mrs. Otis to leave—ever."

"What?" Mrs. Otis exclaimed as she looked from one student to another. "I'm not going anywhere."

"But you might get kicked out the way Mr. Hinkley was," Jessica said.

"Is that what all this crazy behavior has been about this week?" Mrs. Otis frowned. "You all thought Ms. Kovac was going to replace me?"

Jessica felt a prickling all over her skin. "Isn't that why she's here?" she whispered.

"No, not at all," Ms. Kovac said with a laugh. "I'm only a student-teacher. I won't be able to be a full teacher for another two years."

"That's right," Mrs. Otis explained. "She'll be a student-teacher in many different classes first to gain experience."

"Uh-oh," Lila said, her face as red as a valentine.

"But what about Mr. Hinkley?" Todd asked. "He got kicked out, right?"

Mrs. Otis shook her head. "Mr. Hinkley retired and moved to Arizona to be near his daughter. For goodness' sake, nobody gets kicked out around here, especially me!"

Jessica and Elizabeth jumped up, ran to Mrs. Otis, and gave her a hug. Then they both hugged Ms. Kovac.

"Maybe you'll be a full teacher when we get to fifth grade and you can teach us again there," Elizabeth said.

"You think I'd come teach you rascals again?" Ms. Kovac teased.

Mrs. Otis laughed. "At least you've seen the very worst. From now on, all your students will seem like perfect angels."

By Monday morning, things were back to normal in Mrs. Otis's class. Jessica was glad to know Ms. Kovac had gotten a student-teaching assignment at another school. Now there was no reason not to pay attention in class again.

While Mrs. Otis was doing a tough multiplication problem on the board, Jessica heard a loud whisper behind her. "What answer did you get?" Todd was asking Ken.

Jessica looked at Elizabeth, and the two of them turned around and saw Ken show Todd his notebook.

"It's easy," Ken said.

"Maybe for you," Todd said. "I need help."

"You won't learn if you don't do it yourself," Elizabeth spoke up.

"That's right. It's hard for me, too, but I'm trying," Jessica said.

Todd frowned. "Who asked you?"

Elizabeth shook her head at Jessica.

Jessica shrugged. Both turned around and went back to their own work. And both could hear Todd asking Ken for the answer to the next problem.

Will Todd be asking Ken for all his answers from now on? Find out in Sweet Valley Kids #47, Elizabeth the Tattletale.

SIGN UP FOR THE SWEET VALLEY HIGH® FAN CLUB!

Hey, girls! Get all the gossip on Sweet Valley High's® most popular teenagers when you join our fantastic Fan Club! As a member, you'll get all of this really cool stuff:

- Membership Card with your own personal Fan Club ID number
- A Sweet Valley High® Secret Treasure Box
- Sweet Valley High® Stationery
- Official Fan Club Pencil (for secret note writing!)
- Three Bookmarks
- A "Members Only" Door Hanger
- Two Skeins of J. & P. Coats® Embroidery Floss with flower barrette instruction leaflet
- Two editions of *The Oracle* newsletter
- Plus exclusive Sweet Valley High® product offers, special savings, contests, and much more!

---

1 (800) I LUV BKS!

If you'd like to hear more about your
favorite young adult novels and writers . . .
OR
If you'd like to tell us what you thought
of this book or other books
you've recently read . . .

CALL US at 1(800) I LUV BKS
[1(800) 458-8257]

Monday to Friday, 9AM – 8PM EST

You'll hear a new message about books and
other interesting subjects each month.

**The call is free, but please get
your parents' permission first.**